AF345369

Padma Shri Pran

Maurice Horn, the editor of World Encyclopedia of Comics, has described cartoonist PRAN as Walt Disney of India.

Entertaining generation after generation, his comics have been constant companion of all the growing youngsters providing fun and amusement through his famous characters like CHACHA CHAUDHARY, SABU, SHRIMATIJI, PINKI, BILLOO, RAMAN etc. More than 600 of his titles are selling well in the market, and numerous comic strips are regularly appearing in various newspapers. His CHACHA CHAUDHARY comics had already been adapted for a TV Serial, and ran continuously for 600 episodes on a premier channel.

Travelling widely over the globe, he delivers lectures at various International Conferences. He has also been honoured with 'People of The Year Award' by Limca Book of Records for popularizing comics. His comic book 'United We Stand' was released in 1983 by the then Prime Minister Mrs. Indira Gandhi, and is still very popular among children.

Publisher

BOY! DON'T EVER RESIST NEXT TIME.

HEY, PEST! WAIT!

JUST TIE MY SHOE LACES.
BHONDU! I'M NOT YOUR SERVANT.

YOU'RE ARGUING BACK WITH ME?

SORRY, BHONDU BOSS! MY MISTAKE.

WEAK PEOPLE ARE ONLY MEANT TO SERVE.

EVERYONE SCARES A WEAKLING. TAKE EXERCISE TO BE STRONG.
TAKE EXERCISE TO BE STRONG.

NEXT DAY-
JOJI! SHOULD WE WATCH A FILM TODAY?
SORRY! I DON'T HAVE FREE TIME.

I'M GOING TO WATCH A MOVIE WITH BAMBO.

BABY! IS THIS ICECREAM STICK TROUBLING YOU?
NO, BAMBO!

COME, LET'S GO TO THE THEATRE.

ZOOOMMMM

THESE DAYS GIRLS PREFER WELL BUILT BOYS.

WEAKLINGS LIKE US SHOULD BE BUSY IN YOGA AND MEDITATION.

I'LL MAKE SIX PACKS & BE RESPECTED BY EVERYONE.
WHEN BILLO DECIDES, HE DOES IT.

GAMA BOSS! I WANT TO HAVE 6 PACKS.
WORK HARD & YOU'LL DEFINITELY GET THEM.

GOOD JOB! THE MORE YOU SWEAT, THE BETTER IT IS FOR YOU.

I'M BREATHLESS,
BUT I'LL DO IT.

DO IT CONTINUOUSLY 50 TIMES. NERVES WILL GET STRENGTH.

CRACK K !
OUCH!

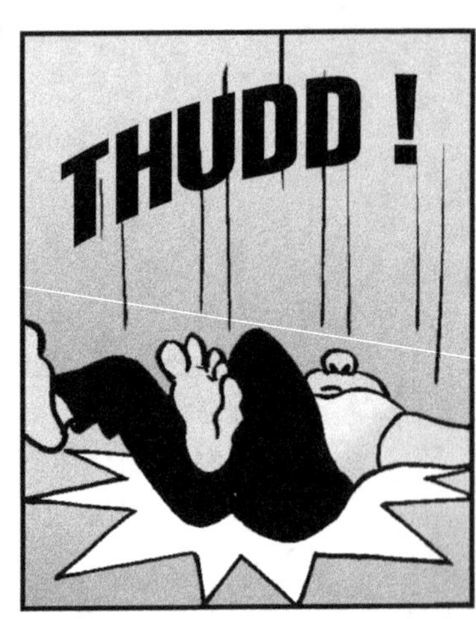

THUDD !

YOU'VE TO WEAR THIS PLASTER FOR 3 MONTHS.

IN THE HUNT FOR 6 PACKS, DON'T LOSE YOUR ORIGINAL PARTS.

PRAN
CHACHA CHAUDHARY
AND
CRISPY'S MAGIC

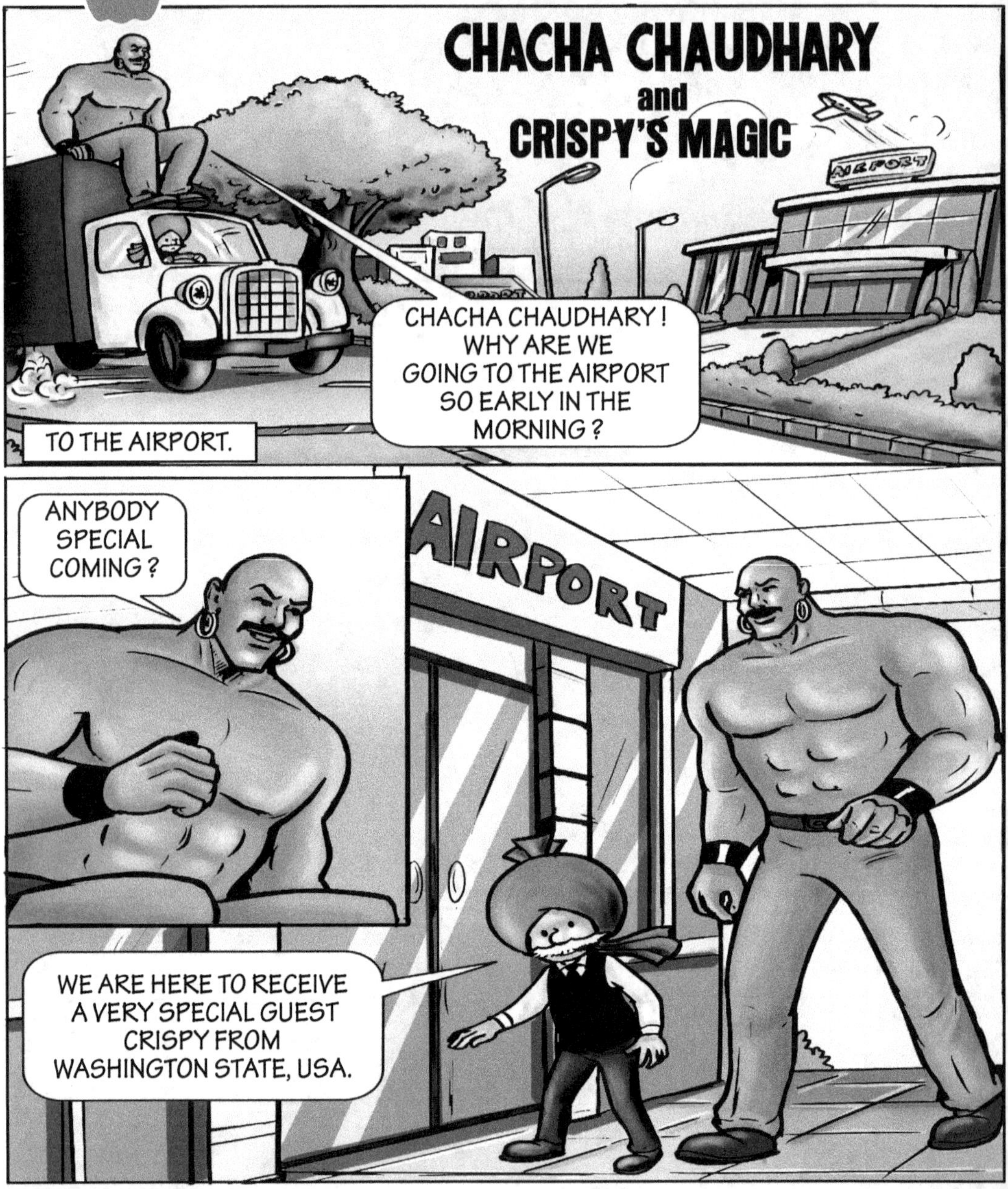

CHACHA CHAUDHARY
and
CRISPY'S MAGIC

I'VE NEVER HEARD THIS NAME BEFORE.
WASHINGTON STATE PRODUCES THE BEST APPLES IN THE WORLD.
LOCATED IN THE PACIFIC NORTH WEST OF AMERICA, WASHINGTON APPLES HAVE MORE THAN 1,70,000 ACRE AREA WHERE THESE ARE GROWN.
HERE THE BEST APPLES OF DIFFERENT VARIETIES, TASTE, FLAVOUR AND COLOR ARE GROWN.
YOUR SECRET TO SHARP BRAIN IS AN APPLE A DAY.
3000 FT ABOVE THE SEA LEVEL, THEY ARE CULTIVATED WITH FRESH WATER RICH IN MINERALS.
WASHINGTON
Tasty delight
No other apple comes close.
apples@scs-group.com • bestapples.com
facebook.com/WashingtonApples.India
twitter.com/WApplesIndia

I'M ALREADY FEELING HUNGRY.
THERE'S OUR FRIEND CRISPY.
WELCOME TO INDIA.

WASHINGTON

MY INTELLIGENCE SOURCES HAVE TOLD THAT CRISPY FROM AMERICA HAS COME TO INDIA.
IF WE KIDNAP HIM, WE CAN DEMAND A GOOD RANSOM.
HALT ! WE ARE GOING TO KIDNAP CRISPY.
WE'VE HEARD THAT YOU HAVE BROUGHT APPLES FROM WASHINGTON STATE.
THEY ARE AT BACK OF DUGDUG.

WASHINGTON
No other apple comes close.

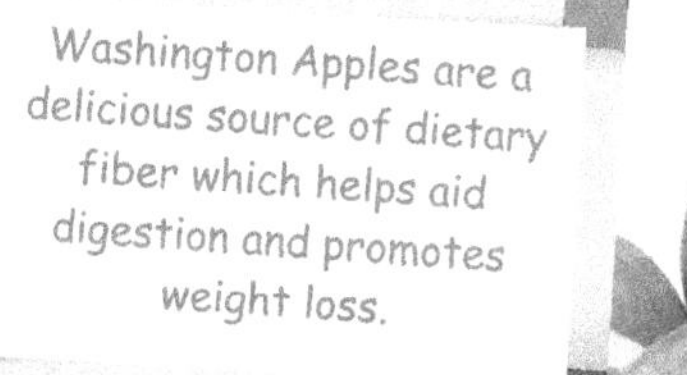

Washington Apples are a delicious source of dietary fiber which helps aid digestion and promotes weight loss.

WASHINGTON

HUBA...
HUBBA !

SWOOSH !

THUD D !

WASHINGTON
No other apple
comes close.
apples@scs-group.com • bestapples.com
facebook.com/WashingtonApples.India
twitter.com/WApplesIndia

Washington Apples
contain almost zero
fat and cholesterol

OHH !
KICK K !
WHAM M !
OWWW !
WHERE HAVE THEY GONE ?
I'LL HAVE AN APPLE.
WELCOME TO INDIA, CRISPY.
DIRECT TO WASHINGTON STATE'S JAIL.
WASHINGTON

Washington Apples

Wholesome health

Healthy eating doesn't get better than this.
Every bite of Washington apples is filled
with juicy goodness.
So go ahead, take another bite!

apples@scs-group.com • bestapples.com
facebook.com/WashingtonApples.India
twitter.com/WApplesIndia

BiLLOO - PAINTER
DHAKKAN- BOSS! WHOSE PIC IS THIS?
THIS IS MY GREAT GRANDAD RAI BAHADUR SHAMSHER SINGH.
AND WHOSE IS THE OTHER PIC?
MY GRANDAD DALER SINGH.

AND WHO'S IN THE THIRD FRAME?
MY DAD, DABANG SINGH.

YOU ALSO GET A SIMILAR PIC OF YOURS MADE.

RUSTAM-E-HIND BAJRANGI'S MAGNIFICENT PORTRAIT.

WILL HAVE TO HUNT FOR A GOOD PAINTER.

PEHALWAN! THAT BILLOO'S GOOD AT PAINTING.

THEN I CAN GET MY PAINTING DONE FREE OF COST.

BILLOO! WAIT!

YOU'VE TO PAY TAX FOR PASSING FROM HERE.

BUT MY POCKETS ARE EMPTY.
THEN YOU'VE TO MAKE ME A WONDERFUL PORTRAIT.

BUT... I'M...

NO IF... NO BUT...!!

OK, AS YOU SAY!

COME WITH ME TO THE ART STUDIO FOR YOUR PORTRAIT.
WOW!

COME INSIDE!

DON'T MOVE! KEEP STILL!

BILLOO! BRING OUT MY FEATURES WELL.
I'LL USE MY ENTIRE TALENT.

TAKE CARE OF MY GLORIOUS MOUSTACHES.

DON'T WORRY! NOTHING WILL BE LEFT OUT.

IS THE PIC READY?

I'M DESPERATE TO SEE MY LOVELY PIC.

WHAT'S THIS? DO I LOOK LIKE THIS?

DON'T DO REAL ART, I DO MODERN ART.

PUNISHMENT FOR RUINING MY FACE.

BILLOO
HAPPY DIWALI
FRIENDS! SEE, THIS STRING OF 500 CRACKERS.
WOW!
THAT'S GREAT!

IT WILL KEEP BURSTING FOR 20 MINUTES.
REALLY?

MY DIWALI SPECIAL LARGE ATOM BOMB.
WOW! IT'S REALLY BIG.

MY BOMB'S SOUND WILL ROCK THE EARTH.
MY STRING WILL DO WONDERS.

BILLOO WHERE ARE YOUR CRACKERS?

HA! HA! SEEMS BILLOO HAS GONE BANKRUPT THIS DIWALI.

YOU'LL GO CRAZY WHEN YOU SEE MY CRACKER. I'LL BRING IT.

SEE MY ROCKET BOMB.

SUCH A BIG ONE?
IS IT CHINESE?
THIS IS, MADE IN INDIA!

JUST SEE MY ROCKET WILL ZOOM INTO THE SKY.

VR
OO
MM
MM
M !

SWOOSHH!
OH, SOMEONE STOP IT.

WHERE DID IT GO?
TO AMERICA.

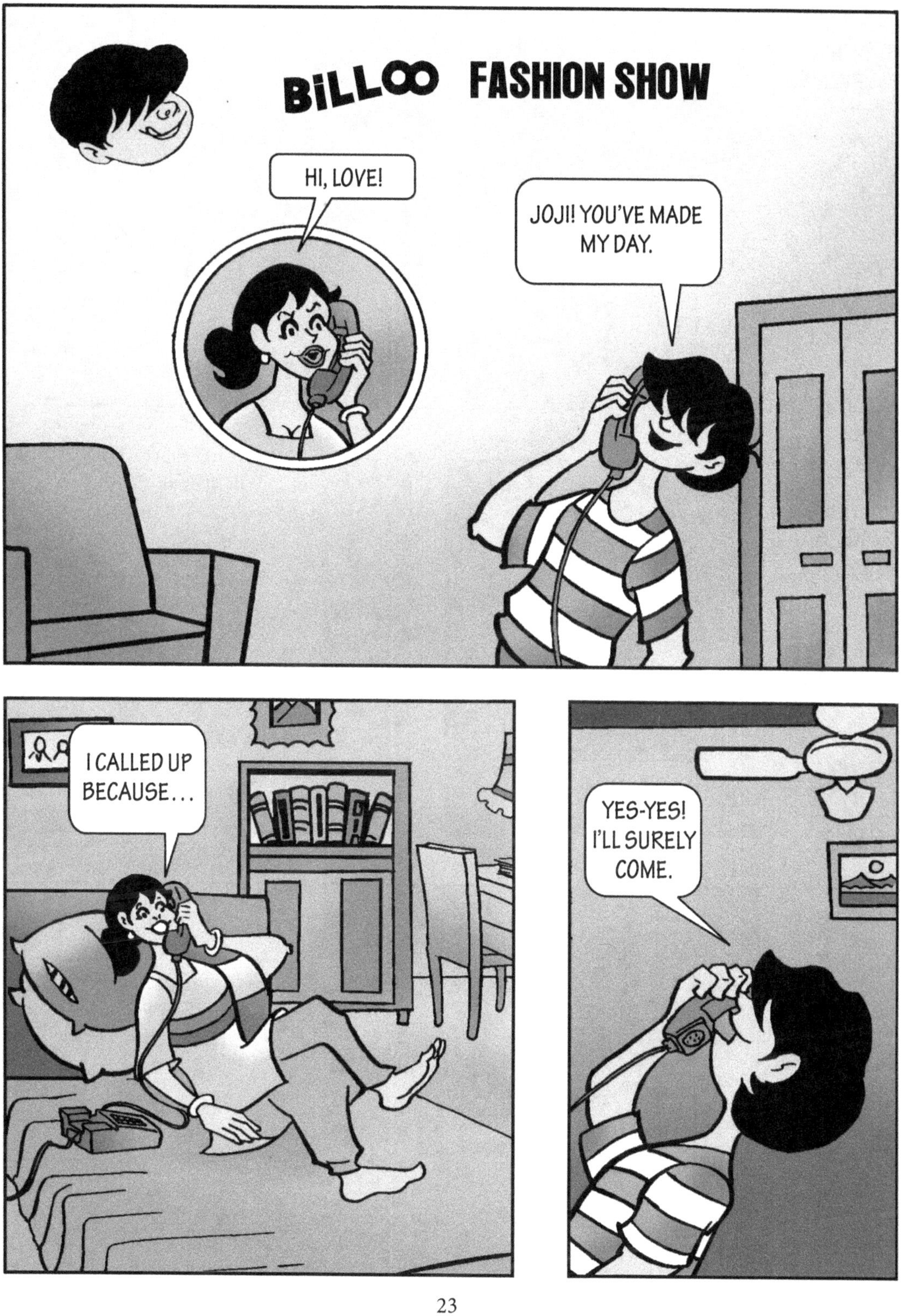

BILLOO FASHION SHOW

IN THE EVENING.

SON WHERE ARE YOU OFF TO?
JOJI IS PARTICIPATING IN A FASHION SHOW.
SHE HAS INVITED ME.

HE'LL EVEN GO TO PARIS FOR HIS GIRLFRIEND.

WOW! TO SEE JOJI'S CATWALK WOULD BE A RARE SPECTACLE.

BUDDY! WHERE ARE YOU OFF TO? IT IS CRICKET PRACTICE TIME.
FASHION SHOW IS MORE IMPORTANT THAN CRICKET.

????

MissWORLD
I'VE REACHED ON TIME. ENTRY'S STARTED.

WOW! PRETTY LOOK!
CLAPPING !

OH! I'VE SLIPPED!
SWISH !!

THUDDD !
OUCH!!

WON'T FORGET THIS SHOW.

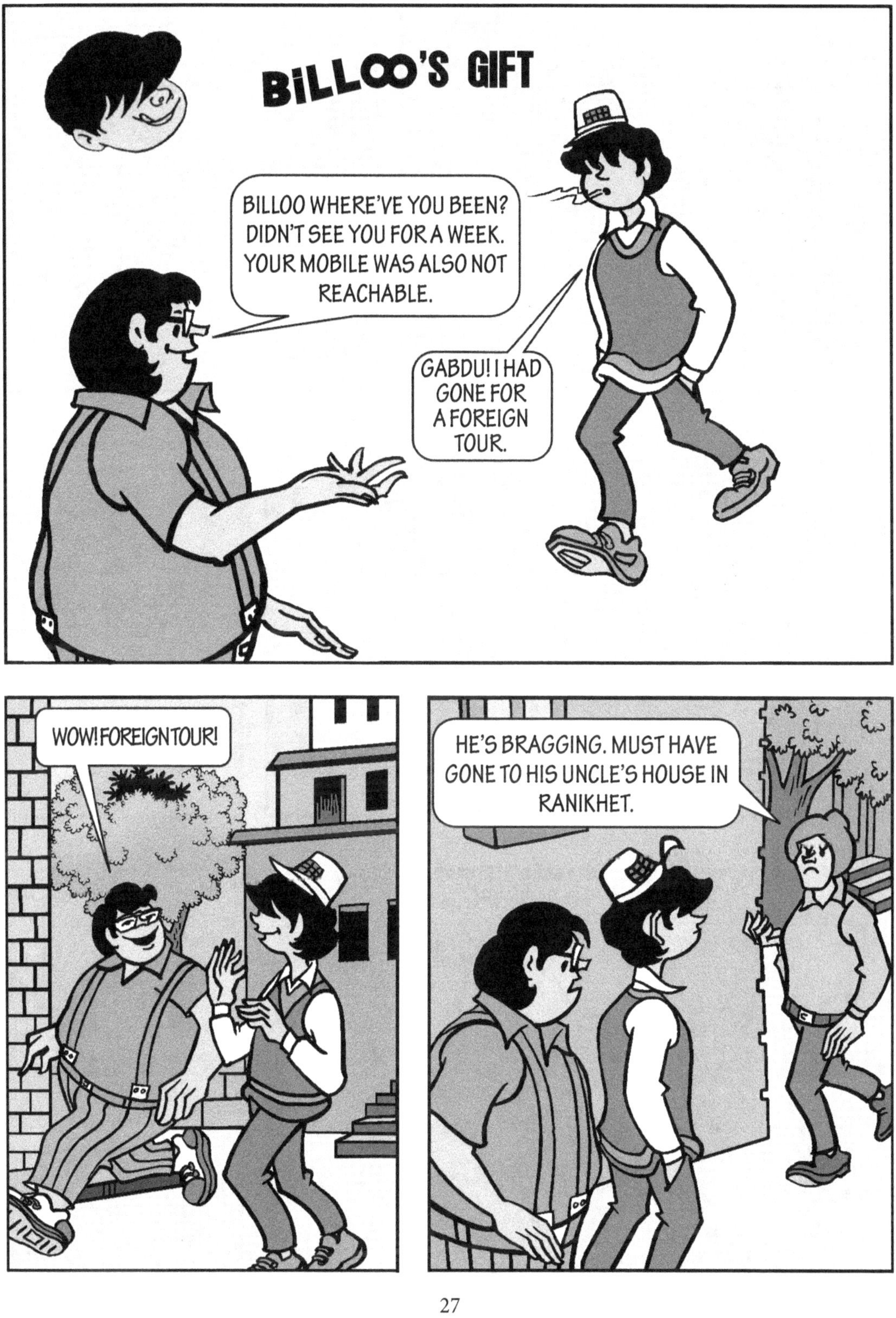

BILLOO'S GIFT

I'M TELLING THE TRUTH.
WHICH COUNTRY DID YOU VISIT?

MY FB FRIEND PETER CALLED ME TO VISIT NORWAY.

HE LIVES THERE IN OSLOW.

TOTAL LIE.

I WAS IN OSLOW FOR A WEEK.
OK, TELL. HOW DOES OSLOW LOOK LIKE?

IT'S GOT HIGH HILLS...

SNOW-COVERED MOUNTAINS AND GREEN VALLEYS.

THERE WAS SNOWFALL. THERE WERE SNOW COVERED HOUSES, ROADS AND TREES...

THIS COULD'VE HAPPENED IN AN INDIAN HILL STATION TOO. MAYBE YOU VISITED KASHMIR.

LOOK, MY MOBILE STATUS.
I WAS IN OSLOW WITH MY FRIEND.

WE ENJOYED PARAGLIDING THERE...

...UNFURLED
OUR TRICOLOR
ON THE SNOW
COVERED PEAK.

...UNFURLED OUR
TRICOLOR ON THE
SNOW COVERED PEAK.
WHAT GIFT DID YOU BRING FOR
YOUR FRIENDS FROM OSLOW?

H &SONS
YES
BRO!

WHEN A PERSON VISITS A NEW
PLACE, HE BRINGS A SOUVENIR
FOR HIS FRIENDS FROM THERE.

WHENEVER I VISIT JAMMU, I GET DRY FRUITS FOR YOU.
WHENEVER I VISIT MY UNCLE IN AGRA, I GET PETHA FOR EVERYONE.
WHAT SPECIALITY HAVE YOU BROUGHT FROM OSLOW FOR THE 2 OF US?

THEY'VE CAUGHT ME.

FRIENDS! I PURCHASED FOREIGN ICE FOR YOU FROM THERE...

WHILE COMING TO INDIA, IT MELTED AWAY.

31

BILLOO AND FLIES

AFTER SOME TIME
HERE! TAKE IT DEAR.

THANKS MOM! YOU'RE GREAT.
DON'T FLATTER ME.

I'M GOING FOR MY BATH.

TAKE COARE IF SOMEONE COMES AT THE DOOR.

MOM FORGOT TO PUT SUGAR IN THIS.

WHAMM!
!!
OUCHH!

OH, HELL!

SOMEONE'S AT THE DOOR.

OH! SO MANY FLIES AT MONA'S PLACE.

CLEAN INDIA CAMPAIGN'S GOING ON. STILL NO CLEANLINESS HERE.
I SHOULD GET AWAY.

I'LL GO IN THE OPEN.

WHOM ARE YOU ESCAPING FROM?
FROM THESE FLIES.

MOVE YOUR HAND WITH FORCE.

GET AWAY!
LOOK! ALL HAVE GONE.

THEY'VE COME AGAIN.
GO TO THE PARK. THEY'LL SPARE YOU & SIT ON THE FLOWERS.

JOJI WAS RIGHT.

THANK GOD I AM SPARED FROM THEM.

OH! THEY'VE COME AGAIN.
THEY WON'T SPARE ME TILL I'VE GOT THE FLAVOUR OF SUGAR ON ME.

I'LL DIVE INTO THE POND SO THAT SUGAR GETS DISSOLVED.

SPLASHHH !

OUCHH! THERE'S A CRAB IN THE WATER.

SO WHAT ARE
YOU DOING?

NET CHATTING
WITH MY
GIRLFRIEND.

BILL∞
NET CHATTING

INTERNET,
ELECTRICITY BILL
AND COMPUTER
MAINTENANCE...

DO YOU THINK
MONEY GROWS
ON TREES?

THESE YOUNGSTERS DON'T THINK OF ANYTHING EXCEPT WASTING MONEY.

OH!

WHY ARE YOU NAGGING MY SON ALWAYS?

IF THEIR GENERATION WON'T DO CHATTING, THEN WHO'LL DO IT?
IF HE WANTS TO CHAT WIH HIS FRIEND, HE SHOULD VISIT HER AND TALK FACE TO FACE FOR HOURS.

HAVE NO OBJECTION ON THEIR TALKING.

BUT I WON'T ALLOW WASTEFUL EXPENDITURE.

LEAVE THE COMPUTER RIGHT AWAY, & VISIT YOUR GIRLFRIEND.

AS YOU SAY.

SWISHH!!

I HAVE SAVED.

NOT SAVING, BUT DOUBLE EXPENDITURE.

HIS GIRLFRIEND LIVES IN BENGALURU.

NOW YOU'LL PAY FOR THE CAR EXPENSES.

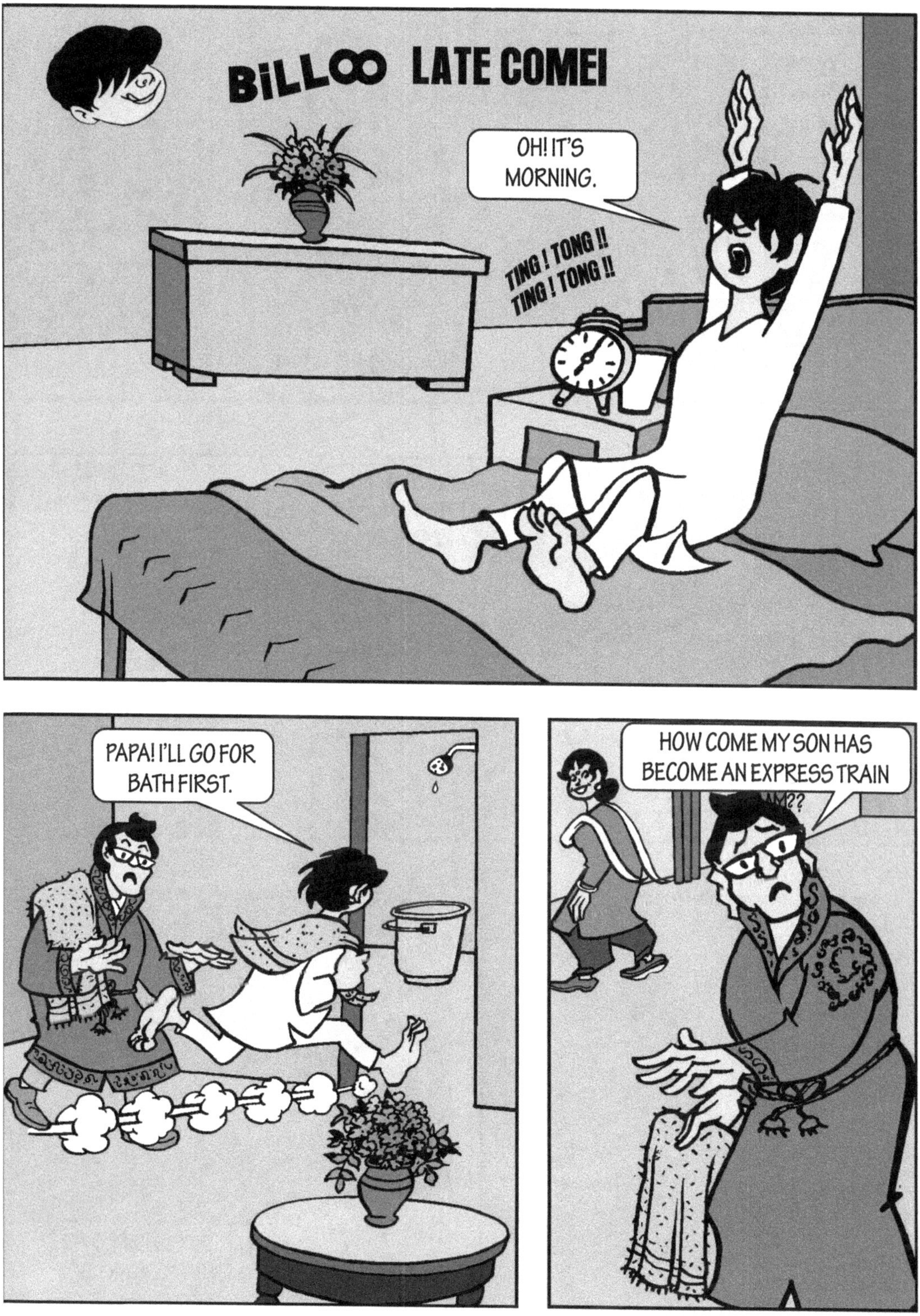

BILLOO LATE COMEI

YEAH! EVERYDAY I GET A SORE THROAT WAKING HIM UP.

THANK GOD IT DIDN'T HAPPEN TODAY.
I AM SURPRISED. MY LETHARGIC SON APPEARS DIFFERENT TODAY.

YOU ARE ALWAYS FINDING FAULTS IN HIM.

BILLO! ... QUICK!!

... QUICK !!
... QUICKER !!
NOW MY SON IS IMPROVING. HE'S AN INTELLIGENT BOY.

HAD I NOT BEEN SWEATING, I WOULD HAVE TAKEN A DRY CLEAN BATH.

MOM! IS BREAKFAST READY?
I'LL JUST SERVE IT.

IT'S STRANGE. REALLY OVERSPEEDING TODAY.

NOW I'LL WAKE UP ON TIME...

WILL FINISH ALL MY WORK ON TIME...

EVEN REACH SCHOOL ON TIME...

THOSE WHO VALUE TIME, ATTAIN SUCCESS.

BYE, MOM DAD!

I'VE REACHED HERE BEFORE THE SCHOOL BUS COULD REACH. NOW I WON'T BE CALLED A LATECOMER.

COME BILLOO I'LL DROP YOU TO SCHOOL.
UNCLE MY BUS IS ABOUT TO COME.

I'M GOING TOWARDS YOUR SCHOOL.
YOU'LL SAVE TIME.

UNCLE TAKE THIS WAY. IT'S A SHORTCUT.
AS YOU WISH.

YOU'LL SAVE HALF THE TIME WHILE GOING FROM HERE.

YOU'RE RIGHT. TIME IS PRECIOUS. WE SHOULD SAVE IT.

TAKE THE CAR BACK. THERE'S A PROCESSION AHEAD.

UNCLE PUT THE CAR IN BACK GEAR. WE'LL TAKE ANOTHER WAY.

BILLOO! MY CAR HAS COME IN THE RESERVE. YOU BETTER TAKE YOUR BUS.

OH NO!!
DL

STOP THE BUS!
I'VE TO ENTER.

IT'S CROWDED. YOU WON'T
BE ABLE TO ENTER.

I'VE TO REACH
SCHOOL AT
ANY COST.

OHH!

SO MR. LATECOMER
HAS REACHED!

YOU'LL STAND ON THE DESK FOR HALF DAY. OTHERS SHOULD GET A LESSON FROM THIS.
TODAY'S DELAY WASN'T MY FAULT.
FRIENDS, STATUE OF LIBERTY - PRIDE OF AMERICA.
STATUE OF A LATECOMER- OUR SCHOOL'S PRIDE!
HA! HA!!

www.ingramcontent.com/pod-product-compliance
Lightning Source LLC
LaVergne TN
LVHW050622200726
843508LV00010B/1967